AM I YOUR NUMBER 1?

Cindi–

You are amazing at valuing your kids, grandkids, and each of your students over the years as your #1! I have learned so much from you, for this I am so grateful. Thanks for supporting my book project. I love you dear friend.

Cassandra Thomas Funderburk, Ed.D

Fulton Books
Meadville, PA

Published by Fulton Books 2022

ISBN 978-1-63985-227-7 (paperback)
ISBN 979-8-88505-763-9 (digital)

Printed in the United States of America

My Mom and Dad who valued each of their children
and grandchildren as their number one.

Love, Your Daughter

Happiness is felt around our house as everyone talks about my new baby brother coming home.

My mommy has carried him very close, but soon he will be here—yes, here…in my room, sharing my toys…my books…my dog, Dixie…and even my mommy and daddy. I wonder if I will still be the family's little number 1?

"Mommy, I have been your number 1 for many years, but when the baby is born, who will be your number 2?"

"As your mom, I cannot choose as things you have done have been your and my first, but your brother will soon have firsts too, that makes you both my special number 1s."

1

"Daddy, who will be your number 1 when my baby brother arrives?"
"Son, as you look into the sky, I see the wonder in your eyes. When your baby brother is born, new wonders will be explored. No wonders are better, you see, so each will be number 1 to me."

4

"Grandma, who will be your number 2? Will it be me or the new little one?"

"You were born first, then your brother second, but my love for you both will always be equal and number 1, so you will both be loved, and we will have so much fun."

"Papa, will I be your number 1 or number 2 when my little brother is born?"

"Dear grandson, you will always be number 1 in my eyes, but when baby brother comes, he too will bring joy. My heart is big enough to love two number 1 little boys."

"Uncle, you always surprise me with candies and gifts. Will I get the number 1 treatment from you when my baby brother comes home?"

"Dear nephew, I have loved you since the day you were born and will love your brother the same. There will be plenty of excitement and fun to go around for you and the new one to claim."

What about my favorite aunt? Will I be number 1 or number 2 to her? She always makes me feel special by reading books and telling wonderful stories to me.

"Oh sweet, sweet nephew... How could I love you less than the BEST? You will always be my number 1."

"But what about my brother, does that make him your number 2?"

"Your brother will also be number 1 as he will be as special to me as you, you see."

Little brother, I am so glad that you have arrived! We are going to have so much fun. The only number 2 in our family will be when we are together…number 1 plus number 1 = TWO Number 1 brothers taking on the world together.

About the Author

Cassandra Thomas Funderburk was born and raised in Tulsa, Oklahoma. She received her doctoral degree in education administration from Oklahoma State University. Dr. Funderburk finds it a privilege to be a mother and grandmother and has gained invaluable experiences and insights from her children, which she now uses to inspire her writings. She has dedicated her thirty-year career as an elementary school principal and teacher to the growth, development, and creativity of her students and teachers. Listening, identifying, then acting to needs of children have always been a priority through her extensive professional career. She believes when barriers are identified and then addressed, learners can soar. *Am I Your Number 1?* is Dr. Funderburk's first published children's book.

CPSIA information can be obtained
at www.ICGtesting.com
Printed in the USA
JSHW061000300622
27676JS00002B/27